SCHOOL. HASN'T THIS GONE ON LONG ENOUGH?

Jim Benton's Tales from Mackerel Middle School

DEAR DUMB DiARY,

YEAR TWO

SCHOOL. HASN'T THIS GONE ON LONG ENOUGH?

BY JAMiE KELLY

SCHOLASTiC iNC.

New York   Toronto   London   Auckland
Sydney   Mexico City   New Delhi   Hong Kong

ISBN 978-0-545-37761-4

12 11 10 9 8 7 6 5 4 3 2 1   12 13 14 15 16 17/0
Printed in the U.S.A.   40
First printing, January 2012

*Tell your teacher that you should get
extra credit for reading this book.*

*Special thanks and an A+ to Kristen LeClerc
and the team at Scholastic: Steve Scott,
Jackie Hornberger, Anna Bloom, and
Shannon Penney. Glad you've all
gotten another year dumber, too.*

SCHOOL. HASN'T THIS GONE ON LONG ENOUGH?

THIS
DIARY
IS THE PROPERTY
OF
Jamie Kelly

HEIGHT: PERFECT

WEIGHT: PERFECT

EYE COLOR: PERFECT

FACIAL FEATURES: PERFECT

HAIR: LOOKS AREN'T EVERYTHING

GRADES: Really quite acceptable if you don't count the classes they are just making us take to be mean.

Okay.
I understand that
if you're just going to
School tomorrow you
might not care that
much but still—

STOP
READING
MY
DIARY!!

Dear Whoever Is Reading My Dumb Diary,

If you're smart, you'll stop reading it **right now**.

Seriously, just think this through. You're probably imagining that I'll never know, but believe me, you'll say something or do something, and that little clue will be all it takes.

And you want to know **why** that's all it takes?

Because I'm another year older, and another year wiser. I've been at this whole diary thing since I was just a little kid. Nothing gets past me anymore.

And I'm smart. *Really* smart. I'm smart like one of those geniuses you see in a movie where they can't figure something out so they go to her and she's got this beautiful head of **not-blond hair** and they ask her to solve the big problem that is facing the world.

And she's all like, "Yeah, I have the solution, and it will save the day, and I want you all to notice how I'm not using the math I learned in school to solve it."

AND THE WORLD IS SAVED, and to show their appreciation, the citizens of the world make math illegal and eventually everybody is going on and on about how they've always secretly hated math and they're glad it's gone.

I'm smart like she is.

Signed, *Jamie Kelly*

P.S. I know you should never call people stupid or morons or idiots. But I didn't *call* anybody those names. I **WROTE** them here in my diary — my private, private diary that I **KNOW** my parents would never snoop through. They understand that I really trust them to respect my privacy, and I understand they would probably really hate to lose that special, intelligent, mature trust that we share.

P.P.S. I know that friends of mine (and friend-like people, also) wouldn't read my diary. Not because they don't want to lose trust, but more because they don't want to lose consciousness.

SUNDAY 01

Dear Dumb Diary,

Mark has 100 grapefruits. If his friend Sean takes 10 and his brother Brad takes 4, how many grapefruits will Mark have left?

This is a problem they asked me to solve one time in math.

The solution was obvious: Mark is irrationally hoarding grapefruits and it's not helping that the people closest to him are stealing them.

They told me I was wrong, but I really believe I nailed it, and they just couldn't accept the fact that making Mark face his grapefruit problem **was** the solution.

Oh, Mark.

YOU did this to him, Math.

Although it's really Math himself that needs to address things.

I, for one, believe that somebody needs to sit Math down in a chair and say, "Math, it's time that you stopped creating issues like this for yourself. If you won't, we think you should start solving your **own problems**, and not come crying to us whenever you want to know the solution to some imaginary drama that you've cooked up.

"Also, Math, you make us do really ugly, contorted faces while we're working on you, and that's just **unfair**."

HIDEOUS MATH FACES

GORGEOUS LANGUAGE ARTS FACES

And here's a surprise: I'm not doing great in math class.

It's not because I'm stupid, because I'm **NOT**. Ask anybody. They'll tell you I'm not stupid.

(Actually, there is a custodian with an eye patch who might tell you that I am, but I was just a third grader at the time and lots of third graders get talked into playing indoor golf by their best friends.)

Adults **SAY** they want you to exercise

But if you knock one of them unconscious they get all upset about it.

A moment of nostalgia: For many people, it's very hard to mention the word **"stupid"** without thinking of one of your very dearest friends.

In my case, that friend is Emmily.

You remember how Emmily's dad got a really great job offer and they had to move, right? Just like that, Emmily stumbled into our lives, and then just like that, she stumbled back out again. (And also, while in it, she mostly **stumbled**.)

I still miss her every single time I see somebody push on a door marked "pull," or bite their own finger while eating, or ask something like, "If vampires can't be seen in mirrors, how do they know if their jeans make them look fat?"

Oh, Emmily, how we miss you.

Stupid, stupid you.

MONDAY 02

Dear Dumb Diary,

Math today.

Mr. Henzy, my math teacher, **still** seems interested in teaching me math in spite of a great deal of evidence that it can't be done. It's kind of cute in a way, like watching a baby try to reach something just outside his crib. A big, mean, boring baby.

See, he gives me math problems, but I know that deep down, I'm **his** math problem. It probably looks like this:

Jamie + number junk = Mathematician

Sure, this problem *looks* simple, but it isn't working out for him, so he gives me bad grades and sent a note home to my parents, who let me know over dinner that they were not happy about it. They've given me until the end of the quarter, in about four weeks, to improve my grades **or else**.

They have no idea what the "or else" is, of course, or they would say what it was instead of "or else."

Like always, "or else" just means "something we haven't thought of yet but you won't like it one little bit." But whatever you do, don't ask what it is.

You Don't scare me...
What's the worst
OR ELSE ya got ??

EAT A BOWL OF BUGS?

WeAR mom's CLOTHES FOR A YEAR??

okay, okay, please please please don't make me wear mom's CLOTHES.

Like I heard about this guy who had this cousin that knew this kid that went to the same school as this one girl, and her parents knew these other parents who were upset with their daughter because of something she did at school or a hospital or at the orthodontist or something, and they used the old "or else" on her and she made the mistake of asking them, **"OR ELSE WHAT?"**

Sometimes parents freak out when you demand to know what **"OR ELSE"** means, and that's what these parents did. The next thing this girl knew, she was waking up in the woods surrounded by seven dwarves. **True story.**

I think that's what happened, I don't know. I might be mixing up two different stories here. Anyway, nothing against dwarves, but it was probably pretty confusing to wake up surrounded by seven of them in the woods.

I'm wondering if four or three would be any better.

That's why I immediately called Isabella because, along with most other things, she is a **well-known expert** on getting notes sent home from teachers.

Isabella's parents have received all of the Five Known Types of Letters Home:

- Your child is having trouble getting to class on time.
- Your child is having trouble completing homework.
- Your child is having trouble on tests.
- Your child is having trouble behaving.
- Your child is trouble.

Isabella's mom has a pretty impressive collection going....

SAID BAD WORD

SPIT

SLAPPED

BROKE SOMETHING

MAULED SOMEBODY

TOOK PHOTO OF

PUNCHED

KICKED

MADE TEACHER QUIT

GRAFF

BIT CHILD

Isabella's first impulse was that I should tell my parents that the teacher had sent the note home **accidentally**, and that it was meant for another girl named Jamie in my class, and that the other Jamie was probably having a pretty good laugh at all of our expenses right now. She said to tell my parents that nobody would blame them if they simply refused to ever read another note from this teacher again or take his calls, seeing as how he can't even keep his students' names straight.

IDIOT
TEACHER

FALSE
JAMIE
(probably blond)

I had to admit, for something right off the top of her head, that wasn't too bad. But I told her that I didn't think lying was a good idea, and she agreed — unless you're certain you can't get caught, of course, and then it's a **great** idea.

Isabella is very giving, so she had a couple other creative ideas for me, but I had to pass on those as well.

Isabella's Additional Ideas

1. Beg teacher to reconsider grade. Promise to do better. Do some Kung Fu to him.

2. Cry and ask for mercy. While he's thinking about it, give him some Kung Fu.

3. Start with the Kung Fu. Just keep doing Kung Fu.

Then Isabella started asking me all about my grades, which was peculiar, because my friends and I don't typically discuss grades.

This is probably because if your grades are too **good**, people will call you a teacher's pet. If they're too **bad**, they'll call you an imbecile. And if they're too **average**, they'll call you some other thing — I don't know what, but believe me, this is middle school. I'm certain that we have come up with some kind of mean name for a person with averageish grades. Meanness is what we do here, folks. It's best to just try not to get called anything.

Middle school has contributed many words to the English language, and in particular, those which promote the **Science of Meanness**. Please enjoy this small sampling.

A kid who brags about his math skills is called an

ALGEBRAT

A very large zit is called a

PIMPLEPOTAMUS

Beautiful blond girls are called

TOO OFTEN

TUESDAY 03

Dear Dumb Diary,

Those healthy brown cereals that are manufactured to improve old people's intestines are the worst way to start your day.

A lecture about your grades from your parents is probably second.

When Dad brought it up this morning, I pointed out that I'm doing well in all of my classes except math.

And Dad was all like, "You have to do well in *all* of your classes."

And I was all like, "Who really needs to be good at math, anyway?"

And Dad was all like, "**I do**. I'm an accountant. It's my job. It's how the bills get paid around here."

And I was all like, "Dad. If **everybody** was good at math like you, they wouldn't have had to hire you. Face it, the less people everywhere know about math, the better off **our** family is."

And Dad's mouth snapped shut like a big old math textbook. He looked helplessly at Mom.

Yeah, that's what I thought, **Math Guy**.

Mom chimed in and said that I needed to start thinking about growing up, and that includes thinking about things like the good grades I'll need to get into college.

I asked her why I even needed to go to college. It's not like I want to be a doctor or a lawyer or anything. Even **foot doctors** probably don't have to go to college for more than a month or two, since they only doctor one small part of people and it doesn't even have guts in it.

She stared me down. "You might not even know what you want to be yet. Besides, one day you're just going to want to be able to tell people that you went to college. I love telling people that I went to college," Mom squawked.

"You could tell them that even if you hadn't gone," I said. "You could tell them anything. Tell them you're an **orthodontist ballerina astronaut** if you want to."

Then Mom's mouth snapped shut and she looked helplessly at Dad.

"She gets this kind of stuff from Isabella," he said.

Foot
Lungs

Foot
Skull

Foot
Stomach

Yeah. I don't think so.

You risk a **lot** when you beat your parents at an argument. Parents have ways to win, even when they lose.

YOU SAY	PARENTS SAY
"I don't have time to clean my room."	"Then you don't have time to watch TV."
"I'm too full to finish my dinner."	"Then you're too full to eat dessert."
"I'm watching TV because they say ALIENS are invading EARTH!"	"Then clean your room because the ALIENS will probably want to go in there."

OK.

OK.

OK.

WEDNESDAY 04

Dear Dumb Diary,

Mrs. Avon is my language arts teacher this year, and she's one of those people with really huge pink gums, so when she flashes her giant smile at you, she looks like a bowl of that strawberry/vanilla/chocolate ice cream after the chocolate ice cream has already been eaten. It's not unpleasant in any way, but you really can't help but notice.

And stare.

In spite of all of that extra gum, she's a great teacher and it's amazing how much different I feel in her class than I do in math.

In her class, I'm a **star**. I like to read, I like to write, and I'm even willing to sit patiently through her lessons about things like pronouns. I have to admit, pronouns were actually a pretty good invention, so that instead of always saying, "I saw King Alphonse Luigi Bartholomew VanFart the Third," we can just use a pronoun and say, "I saw *him*." This saves time, and lets King Alphonse Luigi Bartholomew VanFart the Third (and the other VanFarts) know that we are SO not impressed.

And here's the thing about that: Why is it that people think it's so classy to add "the Third" or "the Fourth" to the end of their names?

Like, Henry the Eighth. **EIGHTH?** That just makes me think that something isn't exactly working out with the Henrys.

The people in England were all like, "We've actually gone through **SEVEN** of these things and we haven't liked any of them. We're up to *eight Henrys* now. We wanted to try a Tony or a Justin, but all they had were Henrys. Ugh."

And besides, you numberers, the rest of us could all add "the First" to the end of our names if we felt like it.

Although there are much better adjectives to choose from.

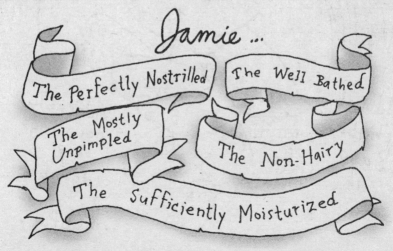

Jamie ...

The Perfectly Nostrilled

The Well Bathed

The Mostly Unpimpled

The Non-Hairy

The Sufficiently Moisturized

Back to Mrs. Avon. I hardly even have to pay attention in her class and my grades are really good. More than anything, I believe this proves that there is something **terribly wrong** with Math. Math should be that way as well.

At first, like everybody, I was all right with Math. It was reasonable. Math and I talked about how many fingers I had, and then later in our relationship, we discussed my toe count.

Adorable chubby Baby me

Adorably counting my adorable toe chubfully

Way back then, 2 looked like a swan, and 5 looked like a duck. 4 was the sail of a tiny boat happily drifting past.

But as we progressed, I saw that 6 and 9 were coiled snakes. Now I realize that I should have recognized that 8, a beheaded snowman, was supposed to be a warning to me.

This may sound like I have a **negative attitude**, but it's hard to be positive about numbers after you learn that more than half of them are negative themselves.

Sure, I know, zero isn't negative, but by now he must have realized that he'll never amount to anything on his own, and that **has** to hurt.

But words aren't like that.

Sure, some of them have made questionable choices about how they should be spelled, but if you aren't certain about how a word is spelled, you can always choose an ~~alturnative~~ ~~alturnitive~~ ~~alturnutive~~ a different way of saying the same thing.

Those sorts of options are there for you when you need to tell somebody who is wearing something gross that it looks gross without using the word "gross." (**Those wearing something gross,** in particular, should be grateful for this.)

So today in language arts class, Mrs. Avon asked us to write a paragraph explaining a short poem that she had read to us.

I finished mine quickly, and then happened to glance over at Angeline, who was writing and erasing and writing and writing and erasing and looking up at the ceiling and then writing some more.

I've probably never mentioned Angeline to you before, Dumb Diary, because her intense good looks, eternal niceness, and towering popularity just aren't something I've ever really noticed. I only mention her now because her Uncle Dan is married to my Aunt Carol, which means we're related but **not really**.

I guess Angeline is a **friend-like person**. I think I would like her more if she was less likable to others.

Anyhow, Angeline was biting her lip and pulling at her luminous golden hair — which is really quite **average** as luminous golden hair goes — and struggling with this little paragraph.

Seriously, Angeline, it isn't that hard. Just write it down and be done with it.

Hey Angeline

I designed a pencil just for you, you dope

At the end of the class, Mrs. Avon asked if anybody would read their little paragraph out loud. I casually raised my hand, but instead Mrs. Avon called on Angeline, who didn't even have her hand up. She must have using some sort of **telepathic prettiness** to attract the teacher's attention.

Since it was pretty darn clear that whatever Angeline wrote was going to be dumb, I inhaled deeply and pursed my lips tightly, preparing myself to make a big, appropriate *ppppffffffffftttt* sound after she read it.

But after she did, Mrs. Avon said it was great and gummed all over the place, and even Hudson Rivers (eighth cutest boy in my grade and known poetry hater) smiled and nodded.

Oh man. Look at all that Happy, Happy gum.

I strongly felt the need to point out that so much erasing went into Angeline's little paragraph that there was a little pink pile of eraser shrapnel under her desk — but then the class ended. Plus, I didn't really know how to make the point that Angeline was only good at language arts through **immense effort,** and for me it all came quite easily, which should dramatically reduce how impressed they all were with her.

sure, planes can fly...

But birds can do it without fuel or flight attendants.

ok. Bad example. flight attendants would be awesome.

Seriously, people. Isn't working that hard a lot like false eyelashes or false cheeks or false eyes? You don't *really* deserve all the praise. Am I right?

All I could do was flaunt my unused eraser as I exited the class.

HUGE Accomplishments my friends should be more impressed with:

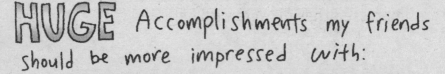

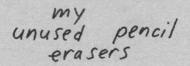
my
unused pencil
erasers

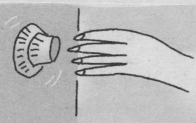
when I hit the
combination
exactly
RIGHT ON THE
NUMBER

when I apply the
absolute perfect
quantity of salad
dressing like a
salad scientist

THURSDAY 05

Dear Dumb Diary,

Today, Isabella was complaining to me and Angeline about being **broke** again. Every time Isabella decides she wants something, we have to listen to her ideas about raising money until she finally gets what she's after.

One of Isabella's Ideas to raise money

Charge her neighbors to babysit their cat.

Charge them extra to reveal **WHERE** she's babysitting it.

Don't worry. I talked her out of it.

Isabella doesn't get any kind of allowance, and we're too young to have real jobs, so cash is hard to come by. It's not like it was when our parents were kids and they could have a paper route or rob a stagecoach.

She told me that she gets as much as ten dollars from her dad every time she brings home a good report card, but she thinks the next one probably won't get her any more than two bucks, and two bucks won't cut it.

Angeline said her parents would **never** pay her for good grades, and I really don't think mine would, either. I wouldn't even want to ask them. I can imagine the huge lecture it would start.

Yeah, no thanks.

At dinner tonight, my parents brought up my grades and maturity again, and I got the impression that maybe they had carefully considered brand-new arguments so that I couldn't **stick them up their noses** like I did the earlier ones.

Dad opened up by saying that I needed math so in case I ever built a rocket or something, I could calculate the right amount of fuel to put on board.

Yup. That was really what he said.

Really.

Mom just stared at him for a moment before she gently eased Dad into his chair and softly put one finger over his lips. It made me think of how you might handle a very vocal and very old ox that you weren't quite ready to make into stew today, but maybe tomorrow.

Yeah OK. yeah. sure. this might happen. yeah.

And then Mom turned to me, and I suddenly had the impression that perhaps I was being considered as another ingredient in tomorrow's stew.

"Your grades *are* going to improve," she said. "You may not believe it now, but I'm telling you, Jamie Alexandra Kelly, either you bring the grades up or the grades are going to **bring you down**."

The sound of my middle name burnt the inside of my ear. I hate it when she uses it that way and she knows it.

"I love when you use my middle name," I said. "Let's use it all the time."

"I know she gets this from Isabella," the ox said from his quiet-chair.

FRIDAY 06

Dear Dumb Diary,

     Isabella reminded me that I asked her to sleep over tonight, which was good because I often forget these things without her helpful reminders. She also just remembered that eight years ago I borrowed a dollar from her. Incredibly, she even remembered that I had borrowed it on a Wednesday. She is **so good** with numbers. I would have forgotten to pay her back.

     Isabella is over so much that my parents don't even try to clean up the house or talk nice in front of her. Deep down, they must love her.

     Everybody knows that the **more** you love somebody, the **less** you try to look nice for them.

Dressing for
Strangers

Dressing for
friends

Dressing for
Family

My parents feel **SO COMFORTABLE** with her, in fact, that at dinner they decided to pursue the grades conversation again, right in front of her.

"So, Isabella," my dad said, trying to sound all sly, "what do you think about grades? Are they important?"

Then he gazed over at me like he was some sort of lawyer who had just asked the question that was going to convict the accused criminal and sentence them to **a lifetime of math**.

Isabella eyed him carefully. I've seen her do this before. It's scary. She can pry open your head through your eyes and see what's going on in there.

One time when we were little I saw Isabella beat up a bully with just a look.

"Sure they are," she said, and, anticipating my reaction, she moved her leg out of the way before I could **kick it** under the table. Isabella is kicked under tables pretty regularly, so she can tell when somebody is going to attempt it just by tiny shifts in their shoulders.

"But improving grades can be hard," she continued. "Sometimes parents don't understand just how hard. There are a lot of things on a young girl's mind."

My mom stopped chewing for a minute and stared intently at Isabella. My dad kept eating and nodding.

I was a little **grossed out** to hear what sounded like the voice of either a counselor or a principal or some similar weirdo coming out of Isabella's mouth — and believe me, I've heard some gross things come out of there.

BURPS.

FART COMPARISONS.

OBSERVATIONS ABOUT EAR WAX, WARTS, AND WOUNDS.

COMPLIMENTARY THINGS ABOUT THE WRONG PEOPLE.

Speaking of gross things and mouths, it was at this exact moment that Stinker and Stinkette (my fat beagle and his fat dogdaughter) decided to bark and fight and growl over some little lump of food that Isabella had accidentally dropped on the floor.

"Better take them outside," Isabella said. I grabbed the **Disgusting Duo** and collar-walked them out of the house and into the backyard.

Fortunately, by the time I got back, Isabella had regained her senses, and we were no longer talking about anybody's futures or **dumb things** like that.

if you are going to own Dogs, you must know the COLLAR-WALK

OINK

FART

GRUNT

OINK

For the rest of the evening, we spoke only of things that really mattered in the world.

Pancakes are the only food served in stacks.

And that seems wrong.

High heel flip-flops would be both elegant

and ridiculous.

Somebody needs to tell geese that they are not that scary to us.

AT NO TIME DID WE PERFORM ANY MATHEMATICS.

SATURDAY 07

Dear Dumb Diary,

Dad got us hamburgers and French fries for lunch today, and Isabella and I ate them while Stinker and Stinkette watched us eat.

It's not hard to guess what they were thinking, because it's a known fact that dogs only have **five thoughts** to choose from.

1. I want to sleep.
2. I want to go to the bathroom and I won't need an actual bathroom.
3. I want to eat what you're eating now.
4. I want to scratch or sniff or lick something and I don't care who is watching.
5. I want to bark until somebody yells at me.

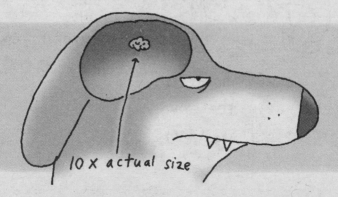

10 x actual size

Isabella likes to torment the dogs by pretending to throw a French fry and watching them scramble for it, which is mean and wrong. I even told her to stop after she did it about **sixty times**.

This antagonizes Stinker in particular, since he is fatter than Stinkette, and for some reason fat dogs are **very determined** to stay fat. My Uncle Lou shares this quality with Stinker, as well as a willingness to fart in a closed car with others. (The Uncle Lou story is long and terrifying. Let's just say that I barely managed to save my own life by breathing the fragrance through the holes in a couple of peppermint Life Savers held protectively around my nostrils.)

I've heard a lot of people say there really isn't a Loch Ness monster, and there are no such things as aliens from other planets, and ghosts aren't real, but I have never **once** heard anybody say that Bigfoot doesn't exist after they saw my Uncle Lou at the beach.

He stayed overnight at our house one time, and after he used the shower, the floor of our tub looked like it had been carpeted.

Even so, Mom loved having him as a guest because he is the only human on Earth who actually enjoys her cooking. Gristle, bone, beaks — he **doesn't care** what you feed him.

"I like anything that will make a fart bad enough to murder my niece, Jamie," he always says, probably.

Isabella didn't want to watch a movie or ride bikes or even do Zombie/Vampire/Goth makeovers, which is usually her favorite thing to do that won't get us grounded.

So since she didn't want to do anything important, we actually wound up doing **homework on a Saturday.** This is when Angeline always does it, thereby turning her Sunday into a weird substitute Saturday. Switching days around that way must have an effect on the **Natural Order of Things.** I'm not saying Angeline is somehow accelerating global warming, but it's pretty clear that nobody can confidently deny it.

ME

ME WITH GOTH MAKEOVER

ME ON MONDAY MORNING

Against Isabella's wishes, we started with our language arts homework. It seemed like the logical place to start, mostly because it's my house and I said she had to **go home** if we didn't.

Our assignment was to write a short poem about life. This kind of assignment is pretty easy for me, since I use words every day and don't feel like clobbering people when I see them (which is the way numbers often make me feel).

Here's the poem I beautifully composed:

Your life is like a pizza.
It could be round, it could be square.
But you'll enjoy it most of all
When it's something that you share.

I let Isabella read it to help her get the hang of poetry writing. Isabella doesn't really seem to care much about words. I'm pretty sure she would be **perfectly happy** knowing only a dozen or so, as long as at least two of them were swears.

I'm so good I would probably be allowed to write only on scrolls

Isabella wrote and erased for a long time until she **finally** came up with this one:

Life is like a pizza.
It is good to eat.
You better share your pizza with me.
You greedy piggy slob.

I stood there for a moment after I read it, not knowing exactly what to say.

I think we can all agree that Shakespeare would have used the word "PIGGY" if he had ever thought of it.

Finally I just **hugged her**, because a hug said it best of all. This was the most amazing poem Isabella had ever composed, and the longest thing she'd ever written that wasn't a list of the same sentence over and over, repeating something she would never do or break or puncture again.

I was so happy I was even willing to **perform math.**

Isabella is pretty good at math, because the things that affect her the most have a lot to do with math: hours of detention, money, how many stitches somebody has to get because of her. . . .

She also keeps precise accounting of the REVENGE she needs to get against her MEAN OLDER BROTHERS

We warmed up on a couple of story problems. The first one was about a guy on a train, but Isabella **switched things up** so that I would hate it less. She turned the guy on the train into Lady Gaga on her tour bus, and I had to figure out when she would have to leave New York if she wanted to be fifteen minutes late for her performance, which is a stylish amount of time to be late, but not **so late** that your fans will start tearing off each other's false eyelashes, or fourteen-inch-tall high heels, or hats made out of banana bread and coat hangers or whatever.

in my math problems, Gaga drives her own bus

In a really fabulous Bus Driver Uniform

Eventually we moved on to our real math homework. It had far less Gaga in it, but seemed to be just a little easier with Isabella there to provide **nurturing support** and **nurturing assurance** and **nurturing arm punches** when I got something wrong.

MEAN

WITH LOVE
I can tell the difference.

SUNDAY 08

Dear Dumb Diary,

My standard Sunday schedule looks something like this:

8:00: Alarm goes off.

8:15: Alarm goes off again.

8:30: Alarm goes off again.

9:00: Mom goes off.

9:30 until bedtime: Wander around trying to not do homework that I know I have to do before bedtime, while avoiding questions about homework and room cleaning and dog-poop-picking-up-from-the-backyard-before-Dad-runs-it-over-with-the-lawnmower-and-creates-a-hideous-Poo-Rainbow-of-Horror.

All pretty much the same color, but still kind of a rainbow

But since Isabella and I finished our homework yesterday, today I was free to **frolic about** on my Sunday afternoon. I was surprised to learn that there were others out there who were doing the same.

This must be how zombies feel when they come across other zombies.

BRAINS.

What? Oh, heavens **YES.** I agree: Brains. Yes, certainly.

Mom and I went to the store to get me some new pajamas, which I am currently too mature to call pj's. Mom wanted to buy me a purse, too, because I always forget a bunch of things when I leave the house, like sunglasses and cash and lip balm and stuff.

The purse is supposed to be an improvement in organization. This way, if I put all of my stuff in it, instead of forgetting a bunch of assorted things when I leave the house, I'll only forget ONE thing: my purse.

just exactly
what do you
put in
a purse,
anyway?

Or maybe Mom's trying to emphasize the fact that I'm becoming **more mature**, and as a young lady matures, her purse increases in size. The same thing happens to men's wallets. It's just simple biology.

Dear Dumb Diary,

Mrs. Avon read some of our life poems in class today. She read mine, as you would expect, and she even read part of Isabella's. (Actually, just a couple of words. Probably right up until she saw the "greedy piggy slob" part.)

Then she read Angeline's:

We write it wrong, so we erase.
And pencil something in its place.
But the words we speak don't work that way,
We write in ink, the words we say.

SERIOUSLY, DO YOU REALLY NEED to WAVE YOUR ARM AROUND when YOU READ ANGELINE'S STUFF?

Okay, Dumb Diary, school has taught me a few things over the years. Once, it taught me the difference between alligators and crocodiles. (Even alligators and crocodiles don't really care. **Just avoid both.**) Another time, it taught me that there are custodians in the world who are too dumb to get out of the way of a golf ball. But today it taught me something new:

The sound my mouth would make if it dropped open to its **widest**, and remained that way for **a full thirty seconds.**

It sounds like this:

I mean, imagine the **planning** it took for Angeline's parents to tell her, the day she was born, to get started on a four-line poem for middle school.

They had to tell her that it should be clever and say something about herself. They had to tell her that she would need to use an entire lifetime's worth of ability in this single poem.

Because based on Angeline's abilities, it HAD to have taken that kind of planning for her to write a poem this ~~excellent~~ adequate.

Angeline looked over at me with her giant grin — really too broad and glistening white for most people's tastes — and raised her eyebrows hopefully. Before I could restrain my disobedient and impulsive thumb, it thumbs-upped her. What can I say? My thumb knows an adequate poem when it hears one.

Note to self: Design gloves to prevent this.

No more accidental positivity!

After class, I asked Isabella what she thought of Angeline's poem. She said she thought it sounded like it had been written by a fanciful fairy queen riding on a silver unicorn writing with a peacock quill dipped in raspberry-flavored ink on a piece of golden paper being held for her by twin baby koalas wearing matching pink sailor suits.

Isabella has said some ugly, horrible things in her time, but even I wasn't ready for that.

Seriously, Isabella. **Nice mouth.**

She also said that they had ducklings and they suck their thumbs.

and had their toenails painted. like little strawberries.

TUESDAY 10

Dear Dumb Diary,

I got an email from Emmily today. You remember Emmily — she was very sweet and we all loved her, but she was not the sharpest knife in the drawer.

Emmily wasn't even the sharpest spoon in the drawer.

Most of the time, Emmily wasn't even in the drawer at all. She was lost somewhere in the bottom of the dishwasher.

And, technically, I didn't get the email. She sent it to Isabella, and Isabella printed it out and shared it with me:

Dear Isabella, and Jamie, and Angeline,

I love my new school. Except the first day I got my jacket sleeve caught in my locker door and had to stand there until this really smart kid suggested that I take my jacket off. I wish she had suggested that earlier so I didn't stand there all day.

I am in an advanced math class and am getting straight A's in it.

Love, Emmily

Emmily is doing better than I am in math?? How is this possible??? Last time I saw her, Emmily couldn't do division because she was concerned that dividing a number was painful to it.

Isabella patted me gently on the head as she folded the letter and stuck it in my purse.

"Don't feel bad," she said. "I'll bet the only reason that Emmily is so much better than you at math is because she has eleven toes, so she began counting higher than you at a younger age."

That made perfect sense to me, but it also made me wonder how many toes Albert Einstein had been born with. He must have had them all the way up his legs. You would think they would mention something like that in school.

I believe I speak for everyone, Mr. Einstein, in supporting your decision to NOT become a SWIMSUIT MODEL

WEDNESDAY 11

Dear Dumb Diary,

Teachers have the **very difficult job** of teaching dumb things to even dumber people.

This does horrible things to their minds and bodies and wardrobes, as anyone can plainly see.

The result is that they have to constantly come up with ridiculous things that make the material interesting enough so that everybody — teachers and students both — doesn't just stand up and walk out of the school because they all suddenly realize that this whole **School Thing** has gone on long enough and, hey, why we don't we all go outside and play in the street and throw dirt clods instead?

Because of all that, my language arts teacher announced that we're having a **Vocabulary Bee** in class. This is like a Spelling Bee, but instead of having to give correct spellings, you have to give correct *definitions* of words.

And to make it extra fair, WE get to pick out the words that will be included in the Vocabulary Bee. Each of us has to turn in three words just before the event, and then the teacher will use those words, chosen at random. I guess that means that even the dopiest kids still have a chance to know at least a few of them.

No amount of erasing and rewriting will help you with this, Angeline. You either know a plethora of words, or you don't.

That's right. I know the word **"plethora."** It means "a large quantity," and we Language Art Geniuses use it instead of "buttload" because "buttload" isn't a very ladylike word to use in your diary.

TURD FACE isn't ladylike either, So I'm not writing that in my Diary either regarding Angeline.

← me. So dignified.

I told Isabella that I'd help her study for the Vocabulary Bee, and teach her the words I'll be turning in. Since it isn't for a few weeks, I figured we could do a little at a time.

She said that was a great idea and we could start right after we worked on our math homework, which she told me that I'd agreed to do — more than two years ago — with her at my house tonight. I didn't have any recollection of that, but like I said, Isabella has a good memory for these things. I've learned that you really just have to **take her word** for it.

Isabella's INCREDIBLE BRAIN Remembers EVERY SINGLE THING That anybody has ever not done for her.

It's all RIGHT HERE

I'm not going to go over the math we worked on, because talking about math you already worked on is exactly like eating math and then throwing it up.

Let's just say that with Isabella's help, I think math may be getting a little easier. It makes me think that if Isabella had been born **Naturally Boring**, she could have grown up to be a math teacher.

I guess if she's ever out of a job, she could **pretend** to be boring.

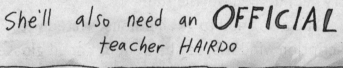

She'll also need an OFFICIAL teacher HAIRDO

The
SCHOOL MARM

Very traditional style for anybody living 100 years ago.

The
E-Z-CARE

A no-maintenance do that you must accessorize with jewelry or be mistaken for a boy or poodle.

The
Bang Blind

Destined to be popular with teachers that don't want to see how DUMB their students are.

Next, we worked on our vocabulary stuff.
Like I said before, Isabella hates language arts,
so I have to choose words that will interest her. Her
word today was:

Mattoid: A person who is only almost insane.

I don't know where I picked this word up.
Words are like that. You read it somewhere, and
years later, you're using it to describe your cousin
Felicia who one time, when she was in a hurry, tried
to dry her hair in a waffle iron.

She also tried to get her house fitted with
prescription windows, so she wouldn't need glasses
when she looked outside.

See? It's almost kind of a good idea, but
also nearly crazy. Just like the word says.

Anyway, Isabella loved the word.

Felicia tried to invent edible clothing once.

She did it by just eating her clothing.

Next, she taught me a word:

Marplot: A dull-witted, bad-tempered rodent of Australia that hunts koalas.

I had never heard this word before, but this is another one of the great things about words — you get to learn new ones all the time.

It doesn't happen that way with numbers.

THURSDAY 12

Dear Dumb Diary,

Thursday is **Meat Loaf Day**. On this day every week, our cafeteria monitor, Miss Bruntford, hovers around the cafeteria like a zeppelin, making sure you finish your lunch. (Maybe I should use **"zeppelin"** for one of my vocabulary words. In case you're wondering, Dumb Diary, it means **"huge fat gross blimp."** When used in this manner, anyway.)

Back to the meat loaf.

We're not here in the summer . . . but some kids are. Some kids go to summer school. (**Oooh**, imagine dramatic scary music, and thunder, and a scream in the foggy distance.)

This strikes me as pretty tragic, not just because these kids lose precious sleeping-in mornings. Not even just because the teachers are probably dressed real summery, and the display of all that extra, aging flesh is surely a terrifying daily reminder of what your future holds.

The real tragedy is that they have to eat cafeteria meat loaf **IN THE SUMMER**.

We've learned to live with meat loaf. They serve it every Thursday and always have, ever since the school opened back in 1492 or whenever.

We eat it, get horribly ill, and recover just in time to eat it again seven days later. We're always within three days of a horrible meat loaf experience. (I can't help but notice how math was **unkindly** ready to point that out.)

But then summer comes and we escape it for a few months, and we live luxuriously on hot dogs and popsicles. Our digestive systems heal and our taste buds cautiously begin to peek out from our tongues again, confident they will not be assaulted by meat loaf.

But not summer-school kids. Today at lunch, Isabella said they have to eat it **every day**, all summer long.

one Summer's worth

See, Isabella has mean older brothers, and one of them had to go to summer school one time.

She says it's always hot and **extra** stinky because the teachers are all wearing coconut-scented sun block with an SPF rating of like, 200, which is basically a coat of coconut-scented white paint. None of the nice teachers are here. **Nope,** the classes are all taught by the substitute teachers that are **not otherwise detained** in mental facilities. Here are just a few subs that we know all too well:

It's a LOVE ROLLERCOASTER, CHILD.

MR. HIPSTER

Quotes from songs that we've never heard.

MAYREE? MAHREE? MORY? MYNEE?

MISS PRONOUNCE

Can't get a single kid's name right.

Bonjour, Class. Welcome to Spanish.
This is science
Mrs. Thepoint
Has no idea what subject she's teaching.
MR. BABY
we think he might be younger than we are.
I'm the Subby-Toot!
Ms. Honeypie
Only the boys like her. And they really really really really really really like her.
Hey shut up, ugly
KATIE HATEY
Can't stand kids. Doesn't even fake like she likes them.

Angeline started arguing with Isabella, saying that summer school was nothing like that, but when Isabella asked her how she would know, she shut right up.

Because summer school only lasts a few months, Isabella said the homework load is **three times** as hard. She said she used to hear her brother cry in his room at night while he tried to do all the homework, and he didn't even cry that much when they had his tail removed, which he still has in a jar and will show you for a dollar.

I'm afraid if I draw the **actual tail** I might owe him another dollar every time somebody looks at the drawing.

Anyway, I was glad Mom made me carry my purse today.

FRIDAY 13

Dear Dumb Diary,

I really feel that my prison for beautiful people idea is going to catch on — and when Angeline is the first one we lock up, I don't believe anybody important is going to object.

See, beautiful people have it made. Everybody loves them. They get everything they want. Eighth-cutest boys in school even trip over themselves when they walk past.

But there is **ONE THING** that beautiful people don't have, one rare elusive quality that has escaped their manicured grasp.

They don't have any **dorkiness**.

Dorkiness may not seem like anything we should brag about, but it's something, and it's ours, and it's wrong for them to steal it.

Today, when Mrs. Avon asked Angeline to read aloud from a book of poetry, Angeline looked back at Isabella and me, reached into her purse, and slowly pulled out a pair of big, dorky **GLASSES**.

She put them on and started to read, but nobody could hear a word she said over the sound of the boys' hearts beating with pure, deafening love.

great. they make her eyelashes look BIGGER.

All of a sudden, Angeline needs glasses.

Isabella needs glasses, too, but in her case, they just help her see things better, like opportunities, and weakness in others.

Angeline, on the other hand, is somehow making them look adorable. **ADORABLE.**

Can you hear me, Dumb Diary?

She took our dorkiness and made it adorkable.

Don't take MY word for it. Let's go live to a conversation I overheard between Hudson Rivers and some of his moron friends right outside the classroom, a conversation that he was not polite enough to have in such a way that I didn't overhear it. . . .

Duh. I am a moron.

Yes. I am as well. I think perhaps all of us boys are.*

Probably. Did you see Angeline's glasses?

I did. I was picking my nose and looked past my finger and I saw them.

She looks so smart.

I know. SO smart. And now all of a sudden we find that very attractive.

So So So So smart.

We are beginning to disgust the world and should stop talking about this now.

* Not all boys are morons. Only the ones that like people I don't like.

SMART? Angeline is smart?? On top of everything else, now they think she's smart.

Hang on one second, Dumb Diary.

Okay, I'm back. I had to go downstairs and eat two bowls of ice cream.

Hang on one second.

Okay, I'm back. I had to lie down because of an ice cream headache.

Hang on one second.

Okay, I'm back. I had to go call Isabella and yell about Angeline looking so smart. Isabella told me that Angeline actually *is* smart, and for some mysterious reason, many people actually like smart people.

You really have to wonder why.

The Pros and Cons of smart People

PROS	CONS
GOOD AT FIGURING THINGS OUT.	MAKE YOU FEEL DUMB BECAUSE YOU DIDN'T.
WILL BE USEFUL IF WE'RE STRANDED ON A DESERTED ISLAND AND HAVE TO FIND THINGS TO EAT.	THEY MIGHT NOT SHARE THAT FOOD BECAUSE THEY THINK YOU'RE DUMB.
THEN WE'LL JUST EAT THEM.	NO CON HERE. WE'LL JUST EAT THEM.

SATURDAY 14

Dear Dumb Diary,

Another email from Emmily. Isabella called and read it over the phone:

Dear Angeline, and Isabella, and Jamie,

Report cards come out in a few weeks but my teachers tell me I can stop working because my grades are so high that they can't be brought down in that period of time no matter what I do.

It turns out there is a secret grade that's even higher than an A, and that's what I have in all my classes. I have that secret-A thing.

I got a Gummy Bear stuck in my ear and had to go to the hospital and now I'm fine but the Gummy Bear could not be eaten afterward.

Love, Emmily

the tragic victim

P.S. Just kidding, I ate it.

Is it possible that Emmily is smarter than I am? Would that mean that maybe **everybody** is smarter than I am?

I spent some time with my beagle, Stinker, and his dogdaughter, Stinkette, today, so that I could feel superior and build my confidence back up.

I performed some math in front of them, and some language arts, too. I have to assume they were impressed because Stinkette paid close attention, and Stinker wandered away, probably humiliated that he can't do math or language.

Also, he **bit** me a little before he left.

I think he is also DEEPLY ENVIOUS of HUMANS' mastery of underwear.

Later on, I went with my dad to the hardware store because it is my dad's favorite place to go to look at bolts and nails and other things nobody needs.

It improved my self-esteem to observe all of the other dads there that were stupid, or extra stupid, or mildly stupid. I know that maybe some of those dads were actually **smart** in real life, but when dads go the hardware store, they aren't really dressing in a way to make you think that.

Still, they all seemed to know exactly what they were looking for, and they seemed pretty happy to find it.

Is it possible that **none** of them are stupid, but they don't care if they look that way? Why would you want to be **secretly** smart?

GENIUS

THE NEXT DAY AT THE HARDWARE STORE

After that, Dad dropped me off at Isabella's to do pedicures to each other. These are fun but challenging, because Isabella is ticklish, so she very often kicks you while you're painting her toenails.

Isabella decided that we should also **work on math**, so that tomorrow we can watch a movie or invent a new beverage or something like that.

I hate to admit it — because I'm against admitting things — but the math is getting easier with Isabella's coaching.

I think it helps that the whole time I was doing her pedicure, she was kicking me **extra hard** whenever I got a math question wrong.

Behold the kick of knowledge

I'm helping her, too. For her language arts, I taught Isabella a new word I'll be using for the Vocabulary Bee:

Smatchet: A nasty person.

Isabella loved this word, and quickly made up a little poem that made use of the fact that **"smatchet"** rhymes with **"hatchet."** I pointed out that it was likely to get her sent down to the principal's office, like the poem she wrote one time about wolves in which she rhymed "babies" and "rabies," or the one she wrote about school that rhymed "destroyed" with "overjoyed."

There are a few words for which Isabella is still seeking cute rhymes...

LUNATIC

tarantula

BARF

projectile vomiting

poke in the eye

SUNDAY 15

Dear Dumb Diary,

Did you ever order a hot fudge sundae, and when it arrived at your table you discovered that it had a bat head in it?

That **exact thing** happened to me today.

Nearly that exact thing.

Isabella came over today and she had Angeline — the bat head I spoke of earlier — with her.

Isabella explained that since Angeline always finishes her homework on Saturday, she is one of the very few human beings on Earth (**other than us**) that isn't busy on Sunday.

And besides, Isabella said that she had a big surprise that she wanted to share with both of us.

Angeline had taken the very clever step of arriving with microwave popcorn, so I welcomed her into my abode. (Those of us that excel in language arts might use the word **"abode"** instead of **"house"** when we want to remind others that they are not as smart as we are.)

We watched a movie about this guy and girl who hate each other at first and then realize they are perfect for each other. During a scene that was uncomfortably kissful, Isabella left the room.

When she came back, she said she had been glancing casually around our kitchen and found a pamphlet about **summer school** in a sealed envelope addressed to my mom under some papers.

Love makes the world Go Around

kiss kiss kiss kiss kiss kiss

But it can also make your stomach TURN

Isabella shook her head and said that it looked like my mom had already decided to possibly send me off to summer school, which made it even harder for her to tell me her big surprise.

But she summoned her strength and told me anyway.

Isabella's parents are putting in **a built-in swimming pool**. It's going to have a diving board and a slide, and we'll be able to hang out all summer long and have people over, and the best part is that it also means that we can exclude others.

I'd get started on the uninvitations already, except that Isabella reminded me of one critical thing:

I MIGHT BE IN SUMMER SCHOOL.

She told me not to worry. We just got back to school and summer is still a long way off. And she said I could still come over on the weekends — if I didn't have homework — and she and Angeline would tell me everything that happened during the week while I was in summer school **learning math** and **eating meat loaf** and **viewing teacher flesh.**

I pulled her to one side and whisperyelled at her while Angeline read the instructions on the microwave popcorn. I told Isabella I couldn't believe that she would hang around her pool with Angeline all summer while I was being tortured in summer school.

She whisperyelled back at me that if I wound up in summer school, it would be my own dumb fault and I'd have nobody to blame but myself.

I told her that was ridiculous because it had always been my experience that you can **always** find somebody else to blame.

The Big Happy Hand

of Somebody Else's Guilt

The timer went off on the microwave and we ate the popcorn while we watched the rest of the movie. I was very careful to not accidentally count the popcorns I ate, as I am currently **very** angry at math.

Corn is great, but Popcorn is better. Maybe we should pop everything:

popbroccoli

popcarrot

popwatermelon

MONDAY 16

Dear Dumb Diary,

One of the best ways for a teacher to tell if his students adequately hate the material he is teaching is to announce a **surprise quiz** and listen carefully to the sounds that they emit.

This handy scale is available to all teachers, and it reads as follows:

Worst Sounds on Earth

1	Marshmallow bouncing off Bunny's face.
2	Opera singer choking on hard-boiled egg.
3	Person you hate singing song you love.
4	Clothes dryer full of horseshoes and crows.
5	Thirty pigs loose in a preschool.

I'd say that overall we were about a **two** today when Mr. Henzy announced the math quiz, although I personally was definitely turning in something closer to a **four**.

There were only four questions on the quiz. When you see that, you're briefly thankful that it's going to be over quickly, but you also know that if you get just two wrong, **you fail.**

Mr. Henzy also always wants us to show our work. This is just bizarre. When somebody makes you a cake, you don't demand that they show you the **broken eggshells** and **dirty spoons.**

You just go, "Oh. Cake. I'll just assume that this contains all its ingredients. Thanks."

I don't believe this sundae exists unless you can tell me how you made it.

I was shocked that, as I was doing the problems, they seemed easier to me than they ever had before. The extra work that Isabella had put into my education (as well as three full-on **facial kicks**) had really paid off.

I guess maybe I'll be wasting my summer around Isabella's pool after all!

For a moment, I thought I could actually smell my baking skin. But then I realized it was just smoke from Angeline's **scrubby eraser** again. Guess this math stuff just doesn't come as easy to her.

mmmm. I Love the smell of other people's dumbness.

We checked our quizzes in class, and I am very **pleased and proud** to report that I didn't smash my head against the desk until I was unconscious, even though that was what I wanted to do.

I got exactly ONE PROBLEM RIGHT.

Fortunately, Mr. Henzy said that these quizzes would not be used for our grades, but they should give us an idea of what the test will look like at the end of the month.

Yeah, I think I have a pretty good idea of what things are going to look like:

TUESDAY 17

Dear Dumb Diary,

Today, at Isabella's locker, we were having a discussion about my quiz performance yesterday and how **disappointed** she was that her efforts on my education had gone to waste.

I pointed out that my grades are no concern of hers, and that I was beginning to lose the feeling in my neck because of how she was holding it.

And then she shouted to Angeline, halfway down the hall, "Hey, Angeline. How did you do on yesterday's quiz?"

Angeline chirped with her typical chirpy chirpiness, "I got all the questions right."

Then Isabella leaned in close enough for me to see myself reflected in her glasses.

"She got them **ALL RIGHT**, Jamie. All of them."

you know, usually I **LIKE** looking at my reflection.

I looked past Isabella and saw Hudson and a few others giving Angeline high fives.

They weren't impressed with how Angeline looked. They were impressed with how Angeline *thought*.

When did this even become a thing? Since when did we start caring how smart we are? I thought we all agreed that we were all some sort of medium smartness and we only made fun of the very smart or the very dumb. And Angeline.

When did we change this??

If I had known BRAINS were going to be so important, maybe I wouldn't have decided to grow up this lovely.

WEDNESDAY 18

Dear Dumb Diary,

Today in language arts, Mrs. Avon split us up into pairs to work on descriptive sentences and I got stuck with Angeline, who couldn't have been happier to have been stuck with me.

"This is going to be easy," Angeline said as she scooted up next to me and pulled her precious, adorable glasses out of her purse.

Not so close, Angeline. MY BUTT Doesn't like you any better than I DO.

"Because you're so smart?" I asked her, broadcasting intense **nasty vibes** with every syllable. (There are five syllables in that sentence, by the way, unless you're one of those people that rhymes "you're" with "sewer" and then it's closer to six — and by the way, stop saying it that way.)

"No," she said. "Because *you* are. You're the one with the big vocabulary. You're **vocabulicious**. Is that a word?"

Angeline is not very good at lying..I've seen her do it before, and she always looks a little awkward, like somebody who is wearing underpants they stole from you and is quite sure that you know it.

She was telling the truth.

You UNDERPANTS BANDITS ARE The EASIEST KIND TO DETECT.

"I'm not sure if 'vocabulicious' is a word, but it should be," I reluctantly admitted. "And I'm not the one that got all the math questions right."

"I think I just got lucky," she said. "I have to go back and check my work a million times. Plus, Isabella has been helping me with it."

"WAT?" I think that was the sound I made. Or maybe it was closer to "WUT?" I meant to say "What?" but it came out in all capitals, and missing an *h*.

"She's helping you, too, right?" Angeline asked innocently.

Sweet kittenish Innocence

Gosh I hate it.

I don't remember exactly what our descriptive sentence was, but Mrs. Avon read it aloud to the class and she held her necklace tightly as she did.

It said something about the enamel on the betrayed girl's teeth splitting as she clenched them tightly to prevent the smoldering rage in her gut from spewing out from between her foaming lips.

It was something like that. Maybe like that, but a little cuter. I don't remember now.

Isabella got the message, and we talked after class.

Isabella is pretty awesome at anticipating questions, and responded to me before I said anything. This is called **Presponding**. (I'm not sure that's a word, either.)

"The only way I know if I'm teaching you right is to help both of you with math. If you both stay morons, I know I'm doing something wrong. If only one of you stays a moron, that means that just *you* are doing something wrong."

I had to admit that was a pretty solid point.

"Currently, you are a moron," she added. "And I'm not sure exactly why, but you are. As far as math goes, you're dumb as a **marplot**, Jamie, and I'm beginning to think you're doing it just to make me mad."

Isabella has accused me of doing many things just to make her MAD.

Winning   Laughing   Ducking

After dinner, I asked Dad if he had ever been to summer school. He said that he hadn't, and didn't know anything about it.

Evidently, Mom hasn't discussed her plans with him.

Not surprising, really. I've noticed that there are several things that Mom just doesn't discuss with Dad:

The Best Length of Drapes

if the bathroom towels should be LILAC or OFF-LILAC or darkish LILAC

if heels should be 1¾" tall or 2" tall

All of the other things that are not meat or sports

THURSDAY 19

Dear Dumb Diary,

At lunch today, I secretly shared another advanced vocabulary word with Isabella. Since she felt like pointing out that I was a marplot at math, I felt I should point out that she's a marplot at language arts.

Plus, without my help, she's going to turn in words like "grenade" and "chain saw" for the Vocabulary Bee — words anybody could figure out.

I dropped a new one on her.

Prat: A stupid person.

It's a splendid word because, like so many splendid words, it's deeply insulting. And it's such an uncommon word that we will probably be the only two people in the whole class that know it.

We've found that we enjoy our smartness more when those around us lack it.

The weird thing about words is that, while we have one as useful as **"prat"** (which everybody would love to use if they knew it), we also have the words **"meat loaf"** (which everybody knows but nobody ever wants to use).

And while we're on the subject, it's Thursday, so it's Meat Loaf Day — but that's just not the problem it used to be. I have bigger problems now.

Other Words Nobody Wants To Use

punycorn

odorpie

squirrelfire

Okay. Some of these aren't words.

FRIDAY 20

Dear Dumb Diary,

I saw Hudson talking to Angeline at her locker today, and I didn't push her down. I am **too mature** for that, as anyone can plainly see by the purse that I maturely carry.

But as I passed, I saw her put her glasses on and I heard Hudson say how much he liked them. I don't think there's anything that says the mature cannot become sickened.

I mean **COME ON**. Just because she's smart at math and smart at language arts and looks smart, we're supposed to believe that she **IS** smart??

The truly mature don't get "GROSSED OUT"

EEWWWWWWW

we get revolted, disgusted, offended, revulsed, or GROSSED OUT OF TOWN

When I got home, I went straight to my room to study.

I warned my brain that I was about to seriously cram it full of all known mathematical knowledge in the universe, and it was just going to have to **deal with it**.

I opened my math book . . . and then my mom shook me awake to come eat dinner.

Seriously. It happened that fast. I don't even know why police bother with tear gas or stun guns.

SATURDAY 21

Dear Dumb Diary,

    Isabella and Angeline were supposed to come over to study today, but only Isabella showed up.

    I was pretty happy about that, since I'm a little tired of Angeline **bragging** about how smart she is, even though she doesn't come right out and say it. When you think about it, that's even worse. It's kind of like bragging about how humble she is at the same time.

    Isabella also made me choke, because when she said Angeline didn't come because she's already smart enough at math, I accidentally bit off my pencil eraser and very nearly swallowed it.

    Note to pencil manufacturers: They should either make those erasers A: less fun to nibble, or B: food.

I wonder if eating erasers makes the other calories you've eaten vanish

My dad checked on us while we were studying, but didn't do his normal routine. It usually goes like this:

Dad: Whatcha workin' on, ladies?
Me: School stuff, Dad.
Dad: Like what?
Me: Math, Dad.
Dad: Like what kind of math?
Isabella: Can you drive us to the mall and wait while we try on bras?
(Then he leaves because Isabella is an expert at making dads uncomfortable.)

But he just looked in, nodded, and left. I wonder if Dad is also becoming more mature.

The effect of the word "BRA" on Dad.

I tried teaching Isabella another advanced vocabulary word, but she says she knows my three and that's all she needs.

She also told me that since I was so awesome at language arts, I could probably stop working so hard at it. I **for sure** had that "secret-A" thing that Emmily is getting.

I mean: I rock at language arts.

Sing (sĭng) v. 1. To utter a series of words or noises in musical tones. 2. To vocalize songs. 3. To create the effect of a melody. 4. To make musical sounds. 5. To make a hum. 6. To praise something. YEAH!!!

SUNDAY 22

Dear Dumb Diary,

Only two moms in history have ever shouted this at the top of their lungs in the living room: **"Pablo Picasso! Pablo Picasso!"**

One of them was, of course, his mother, Mrs. Picasso. She probably had a very good reason for this, such as his little square-looking dog leaving his little cube-shaped bones all over for her to trip on. (She was probably prone to tripping, anyway, what with her backward legs and her eyes on sideways. At least, that's what she looks like in his paintings.)

But in MY mom's case, she was yelling out the answer to some quiz show that she and my dad were watching on TV. (She was right: The answer was Picasso.)

They were laughing and shouting and trying to prove to each other how smart they were about stuff like oceans (the Pacific is the largest), and how Julius Caesar was stabbed (they got him right in the middle of his important duties).

I was watching them in amazement for a moment, enjoying themselves. Then the next question was **"What is a mattoid?"** They just looked at each other, and I answered the question without really thinking.

"It's an almost-insane person, like Cousin Felicia. Remember when she tried to train worms because she believed if they would just work a little harder, and apply themselves, they could be snakes?"

The host on the TV confirmed my answer.

Mom and Dad just sat there, staring at me for a moment.

As their eye lasers beamed into my face, I felt the need to clarify. "I didn't say I thought that worms could be snakes. Felicia did."

"No, no," my mom said with a **huge smile**. "We're just impressed. I didn't know what the word meant."

"She's so smart," my dad said, grinning and turning his attention back to the TV.

Huh.

Surprisingly, it turns out that merely **knowing something** can be pleasant. Reaching into your head and finding an answer is like reaching into an old coat pocket and finding money you forgot about.

I'm beginning to wonder if knowing other things is as pleasant. Except not math. I mean, let's not **push our luck** here.

I've decided to experiment with knowledge by knowing these things:

Coulrophobia is the fear of CLOWNS.

A koala weighs about as much as 5 gallons of ice cream.

Your body contains between 2 and 9 pounds of BACTERIA.

Okay let's all forget about the bacteria.

MONDAY 23

Dear Dumb Diary,

Dad drove me to school today, but he wanted to stop for a large coffee at this place that tells you the size in Italian if you pay them a dollar more than it's worth. **Grande?** That will be one extra dollar, please.

The coffee place had a new guy who could actually get Dad's order right on the first try instead of after three or four tries like the old guy, so that meant I got to school early.

I hate when the school is empty like that, because it feels very much like a scary movie just before something terrible starts attacking the pretty star of the film — and let's face it, I'm pretty **attackable**.

Large

$ 5.00

Grande

$6.00

On a bench, all by herself, I spotted Angeline reading something so intensely I figured it must have been a stolen love note that was probably intended for somebody with **browner hair**.

As I got closer, I could tell that it was just our math book. She seemed so interested, it made me think that maybe the publishers had accidentally included something disturbingly inappropriate.

Angeline and her MATH BOOK

The last time I saw this kind of FOCUS, it involved Uncle Lou and some RIBS

And then I realized that Angeline was cheating on our upcoming math test. Well, she was **kind of** cheating. It's that kind of cheating where you write down all of the answers inside your head. I think some people call this **"studying."**

Can you believe it, Dumb Diary?

Angeline wants so badly for people to believe that she's smart that she is actually willing to **really become smart** just to continue the masquerade. Ugh.

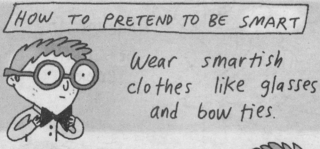

HOW TO PRETEND TO BE SMART

Wear smartish clothes like glasses and bow ties.

Study hard your entire lifetime to know everything.

Knowing everything is a great way to fool people into thinking you're smart.

TUESDAY 24

Dear Dumb Diary,

Emmily emailed me directly this time.

Dear Jmaie,

Sorry it has taken me so long to write you.
My new school is great but I really miss you and
Angeline and that mean boy with the round glasses
that you always hang around with.

Myabe you guys can come and visit me some time
or I can come and visit you or we can visit each
other at some place exactly halfway between us.

Love, Emmily

P.S. I miss you and Angeliine and that mean boy with
the round glasses.

I really wonder how Emmily recalls things

I was pretty surprised. Not that Emmily was remembering Isabella as a boy. (People do that more often than you might think.) I was surprised she wasn't going on and on about her grades like she has in all her other letters.

Maybe she's just so used to being smart now that she's **forgotten** that she is smart.

Even somebody as smart as I AM occasionally forgets how SMART I am....

Enters room for very important reason.

 Instantly forgets why I entered room.

Asks question like somebody with recent severe head injury

 Does CLAUSTROPHOBIA have something to do with SANTA?

Starts third panel in cartoon.

 Instantly forgets memory joke I was going to tell.

WEDNESDAY 25

Dear Dumb Diary,

Today was the **Vocabulary Bee**. Here's how Mrs. Avon set it up: We all turned in our three words, and then she went around the class calling on us, choosing words at random from the ones we turned in. If you couldn't define the word, you were out. If you could, you stayed in.

A few kids were taken out early, and with words that weren't really that hard, like **"stethoscope"** and **"catapult"** and **"chrysanthemum."**

Mike Pinsetti's snorts clued us in to which words he had turned in, although I was hardly surprised that he had submitted "toilet," "toiletry," and "toilet fixer guy." (That was **three** words, of course, but Mrs. Avon just wanted to get it over with. By the way, the word you were struggling for, Pinsetti, was **"plumber."**)

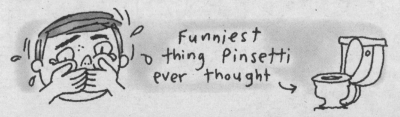

Funniest thing Pinsetti ever thought →

I guess there were no surprises until it was Angeline and her glasses' turn. Mrs. Avon asked her the meaning of **"smatchet."** Imagine my delight when I realized Angeline was going to have to face **MY** words!

Again, I had prepared my long *pppfffttt*. And Angeline answered prettily.

"An unpleasant person."

I discharged only the first two *pp*'s in my *pppfffttt* when I realized she had it right.

Then she got **"prat"** and even **"mattoid"** right. **MY** mattoid.

My mind was reeling. Could she really be that smart? I looked at Isabella, who just threw her arms up in a big **I Don't Know** pose.

Then it was my turn. Easy stuff: **"swindle"** (to cheat somebody) and **"incarcerated"** (to be put in jail). Clearly, these were Isabella's words.

Then came **"marplot."**

"It's a small, bad-tempered Australian animal," I said.

Mrs. Avon giggled a little.

"Wrong," she said.

No, I **wasn't** wrong. And I let her know.

"It's a small, stupid, bad-tempered animal. It hunts koalas. It's from Australia. I'll bet you anything," I protested.

Mrs. Avon laughed.

"That's wrong, Jamie."

I asked her to double-check, and she tapped the word into the dictionary software on her laptop. She read the screen and shook her head.

"You're wrong, Jamie. I'm afraid you're out. Anybody else want to tell us what it means?"

"It's a person that ruins somebody's plans," Angeline said.

"Exactly," Mrs. Avon said, and displayed about four extra inches of gums as she did.

I felt my face go red and then the class had a good laugh and it went redder. Isabella gave me the big **I Don't Know** arms again, and I had to sit there while Angeline went through two more rounds before she finally got knocked out. **I don't even remember who won.** Either that one kid I hate or that other kid I hate.

Mrs. Avon, I love you but I could do with a little less pink.

So Isabella was wrong about **marplot**. That's to be expected, especially when it involves an animal. She divides the animal kingdom into three categories: ones you eat, ones you ride, and ones you throw sticks at.

But I should have known.

I didn't feel embarrassed, exactly. You know how before I said that knowing something was like reaching into a pocket and finding money? This was like reaching into your pocket expecting money and finding half an old taco — and it's not even your taco.

Simply **not knowing something** doesn't feel bad. Things you don't know are just pockets you haven't put anything in yet.

It's **dumbness** that feels bad. Dumbness is finding that old taco.

I can't write any more now, Dumb Diary. I have a math test to study for.

NOM NOM
NOM
NOM NOM
NOM

Studying is like eating school meat loaf with your head.

I may not WANT to DO it, BUT I CAN DO it.

THURSDAY 26

Dear Dumb Diary,

The **big hairy math test** was today. The numbers came at me from all sides. I remember, in particular, a seven that quite clearly had murder in its eyes.

I felt like I got a lot of the questions right. Maybe even most of them.

When I was all done, I detected a fragrance in the air — the smell of burning rubber. And then I became aware of a soft scrubbing sound.

I looked over and saw that Angeline was erasing something and **smiling**. But I could tell she wasn't even erasing a problem. She was just erasing on her desk.

The eraser smell made me wonder if I should go back and check anything.

So I did, and I found **two things** I would have gotten wrong. Was Angeline erasing just to remind me? Was she trying to remind the whole class? Or is she just some kind of a **mattoid** that likes to rub down erasers?

FRIDAY 27

Dear Dumb Diary,

Mr. Henzy worked hard to get our math tests graded fast. Evidently, he has two kids at home that really enjoy math and like to help grade papers. I can hardly imagine how **boring** their dinner conversations must be.

As Mr. Henzy was handing the graded tests back, I felt exactly like a prisoner in some sort of medieval dungeon where the main torture guy is walking around handing out the torture method he had planned for each individual.

(I'm not sure if this is how they **actually** did it. They don't teach us a lot about medieval torture at school.)

"Here you go, son, we've decided to torture you by rubbing you with raw bacon and letting beagles eat you to death," Mr. Henzy said as he handed one of the prisoners the paperwork associated with being **beagled to death**.

"And for you, young man, we think that perhaps stapling you to the wall with our medieval staplers seems like a good idea. Here's your paperwork." (Medieval staplers were much larger back then than they are today.)

And then Mr. Henzy, the **Head Torture Guy**, turned to me.

"Jamie Kelly. Yes, here it is. . . ."

"Nice work, Jamie. You pulled yourself up one whole letter grade with this test," he said.

And everybody turned to look at where the big celebratory WOOOO-HOOOO came from.

For a second, I assumed it came from inside my mouth. But it didn't.

It came from inside Isabella's. It was the first time Isabella ever got excited about a test — and it wasn't even hers!

I think maybe Isabella is **growing up**, too.

Dinner was great. My math test wasn't perfect, and my math grades aren't perfect. But my parents were really impressed that I had worked hard enough to improve.

I feel like a nerd admitting it, but I was actually **kind of proud** that I improved the grade a little. Don't tell anyone, Dumb Diary.

Maybe they teach us things like math to show us that, if we can learn something as unpleasant as math, we can probably learn **anything**.

The grades are just there to give us an idea of how much of the stupid stuff we've learned.

Behold! You have learned your enemy, MATH. This means that you can learn any stupid thing in the world!

Thank you, Oh, KING OF EDUCATION. WHY ARE you Dressed So weird?

NO IDEA. You DREW ME.

KING OF EDUCATION

SATURDAY 28

Dear Dumb Diary,

Angeline came over today. She opened her purse and handed me her glasses. She insisted that I try them on.

"These don't do anything for me," I said.

"They don't do anything for anybody. They're fake," she confessed.

AH-HA! She was only wearing them to try to look adorable! She's not actually adorable at all! What a fake. Wait. She actually *is* adorable. What is . . . I don't even understand. . . .

Angeline could see that I was speechless.

"Isabella asked me to wear them," she said.

"WAT?"

I don't really have a mirror this pretty but I want one

"It was all to keep you out of summer school. Isabella had this dumb idea that it would make you nuts if people thought I was smart. As if you'd ever be jealous of me," Angeline said.

"Yeah. Right. Like. I could. Ever. Be. Jealous of. You. Angeline," I said in a totally convincing way.

"She said that if we made you work hard enough, your parents wouldn't send you to summer school. I was just trying to help."

"*Isabella,*" was all I could say.

seriously, Angeline, who on Earth would ever be jealous of your good LOOKS AND BRAINS AND HARD WORK AND NICE PERSONALITY AND ALL THAT JUNK

"Summer school isn't even that bad anyway," Angeline said. "I went."

"WAT?"

"School is hard for me, Jamie. I know it usually comes easy for you, but not for me. I have to study and work like crazy. You probably don't notice, but I'm erasing and correcting myself all the time. I got way behind one year, so I took summer school classes to catch up. It wasn't fun, but it's not anything like Isabella says. And it helped."

When I finally figured out how to make my tongue work again, I asked **why** the grades were important to her. For a second, it looked like I had asked something I shouldn't have.

"You know what my Uncle Roy's job is?" she asked.

For a moment I wondered if they had the same hair.

"It's —" she started to tell me, and then she stopped herself. "Well, never mind what it is. He's really smart and funny and there's nothing wrong with what he does, but he always says that he wishes that he had worked a little harder in school and had been able to go to college, so he could have had more things to choose from. I want more to choose from, too."

So this was maturity, huh? Talking about career choices? **Ah, yes.** It was suddenly so clear to me why I **didn't like it.**

Angeline told me I could have the glasses if I wanted them, but I passed. There was no telling when she would need to look **extra-super-adorable** again.

We talked more, and I discovered that Isabella had been quizzing her on the words for the Vocabulary Bee. That's how she knew some of the crazy-hard words like "smatchet" and "prat." And she knew what "marplot" meant. For some reason, Isabella had told her the real meaning of "marplot," and not me.

I thanked Angeline for helping me get a better math grade. Not by faking me out with glasses, but by sending up her little eraser smoke signals. She laughed and admitted that she had hoped it would send a message.

As she was walking out, she stopped and turned in the doorway.

"My uncle," she said. "I don't want you to think I'm ashamed of him. I love him and he does a great job, and I'm proud of his work — so is he. It's just that he wishes he'd had more choices."

I told her that **I understood.**

whenever I
tell people that
I understand, I
nod gently with my
eyes closed to let
them know that
I probably do.

"And it doesn't help that, a few years ago, **some kid almost took his eye out with a golf ball,** but that's a long story."

WAT?

I told Angeline that I had never heard of a janitor getting hit in the eye with a golf ball, and closed the door firmly behind her. She may have still been talking when I did.

*Maybe it wasn't me. I'll bet that **TONS** of janitors have been injured by golf balls.*

SUNDAY 29

Dear Dumb Diary,

I left messages three times yesterday for Isabella to call me back. She never did. She just showed up this morning.

"I have you all figured out," I told her as she walked in.

"You do, huh?" she asked. "Is your dad home?"

I ignored her and went on. "Thanks," I said **unthankfully**, "for giving Angeline all the words for the Vocabulary Bee. What was the deal with **'marplot'**? And by the way, Angeline told me about the glasses."

"Relax," she said. "Your math grade went up. All that stuff I did, with summer school, and Angeline, and Emmily — you should be thanking me."

Wait a second.

Isabella feels that you should always express your gratitude to her

It was suddenly clear.

Isabella faked the whole summer-school thing. My parents weren't looking into summer school. She made up those emails about Emmily getting good grades. It was all just to motivate me to work harder.

Isabella did all of this just to help me improve my grades. She did all of this **just so I could feel good about myself.** Can you imagine her working that hard just so I could feel better??

She really does have a heart of gold.

One day I will carve a beautiful sculpture of Isabella wearing something flowy because beautiful people always pose for sculptures in flowy outfits.

ISABELLA THE NICE

"So, Mr. Kelly," Isabella said as my dad walked into the room. "About our deal . . ."

My dad nodded, pulled out his wallet, and handed Isabella a ten-dollar bill.

WAT?

"What deal?" I asked.

"Isabella and I made a deal," he said. "If she could get you to pull up your math grade, I'd pay her **ten dollars**. She has a lot of influence over you, Jamie. Sometimes I think she has more influence over you than I do. She may have more influence over you than *you* do. So I figured that would work better than me paying you for the grade. And it did."

Dad gave Isabella a big thumbs-up and left the room.

GRAB

I plopped down hard on the couch. I felt just like that guy in that movie when he discovered that the thing about the stuff wasn't what everybody thought.

"But why did you try to sabotage me in the Vocabulary Bee?" I asked Isabella.

Isabella grinned, and something resembling pride flashed across her face.

"Because you rock at language arts. There was no way I could ever hope to get your grade up in language arts. Unless —"

Isabella took a long, deep inhale along the edge of the ten-dollar bill.

"Unless what?" I said.

"Unless I pushed it down **first**. I hoped I could hammer your grade down this marking period, knowing you would pull it back up all by yourself next quarter once you thought that Angeline was better than you. Then I could cash in on your dad again. I was just thinking ahead a little bit, Jamie. You can't be mad at me for that."

SQUERSH

"So, you did all of this for ten dollars? You didn't do it just to help me?" I asked her. I was sure she could tell I felt hurt.

"**OF COURSE NOT**," she said, waving her arms around. "I was hoping for twenty dollars. You know, if the language arts thing had worked out."

"But, Isabella, I'm your *best friend*," I choked.

She nodded. "My bestest bestest best friend, Jamie. And that's why if something I'm doing for myself benefits you in some way, I'm totally okay with that. I got my money. You got your grade. See? Best friends."

That actually **was** pretty nice for Isabella, I guess. And, after all, she **did** help me.

"What did you want the money for, anyway?" I asked her.

"A purse like yours," she said. "But ten bucks still isn't enough money. I'll need three times this much."

"Were you lying about the pool, too?" I asked her.

"I was pretty surprised you believed that one," she said with a laugh.

"You can have my purse," I said. "For fifteen bucks."

"Five," she said.

"Forget it," I said. "I'll keep it."

"Okay, ten," she said. "But hurry up, my mom's waiting in the car."

Seriously. She had her mom waiting while she came to conduct her business meeting with my dad.

I pulled my stuff out of my purse, and she grabbed it and headed out the door, smiling broadly. I have to admit, Isabella **is** pretty smart.

So So So So So So So So SMART

But then again, at the end of the day, I'm the one with the good grades **and** ten bucks, and she's the one with a purse that smells like the **meat loaf** I've been putting in it for three weeks.

Maybe I'm a little smarter than I thought. Thanks for listening, Dumb Diary.

Vocabuliciously,

Jamie Kelly

Are You Vocabulicious?

Sing (sĭng) v. 1. To utter a series of words or noises in musical tones. 2. To vocalize songs. 3. To create the effect of a melody. 4. To make musical sounds. 5. To make a hum. 6. To praise something. YEAH!!!

1.) plethora
   a. a very small amount
   b. like a shmethora, but different
   c. a toxic ingredient in meat loaf
   d. a large quantity

2.) mattoid
   a. a person who is only almost insane
   b. something shaped like a mattress
   c. an android named Matt
   d. a reliable person

3.) marplot
   a. a dull-witted, bad-tempered rodent of Australia that hunts koalas
   b. a person that ruins somebody's plans
   c. a plethora of marps
   d. a burglar

4.) zeppelin
   a. a huge, fat, gross blimp
   b. when your zeppel isn't out
   c. a type of helicopter
   d. a word invented to make babies laugh

5.) smatchet
   a. a small hatchet
   b. a type of purse
   c. a nasty person
   d. a shoe made of ham

6.) abode
   a. house
   b. an office building
   c. what a person with a cold gives their dog
   d. also a shoe made of ham

7.) prat
   a. a genius
   b. an adorably small fart
   c. a brat that likes to mispronounce words
   d. a stupid person

8.) swindle
   a. to cheat somebody
   b. to purchase something
   c. a fish
   d. to wear French underpants

9.) incarcerated
   a. to catch on fire
   b. to be put in jail
   c. to be put inside a car
   d. to be forced to wear ham shoes

TURN THE PAGE FOR A SPECIAL
SNEAK PEEK OF JAMIE KELLY'S NEXT
TOP SECRET DIARY....

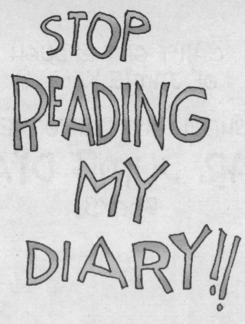

STOP READING MY DIARY!!

Whatever you do, **don't** look for my new diary,

DEAR DUMB DIARY YEAR TWO #2: THE SUPER–NICE ARE SUPER–ANNOYING!

I mean it! I'm older, I'm wiser — and I'm onto you.

I only suspect everybody.

CAN'T GET ENOUGH
OF JAMIE KELLY?

CHECK OUT HER OTHER
DEAR DUMB DIARY
BOOKS!

candy apple

Read them all!

Life, Starring Me!

Callie for President

Drama Queen

I've Got a Secret

Confessions of a Bitter Secret Santa

Super Sweet 13

The Boy Next Door

The Sister Switch

Snowfall Surprise

Rumor Has It

The Sweetheart Deal

The Accidental Cheerleader

The Babysitting Wars

Star-Crossed

Accidentally
Fabulous

Accidentally
Famous

Accidentally
Fooled

Accidentally
Friends

How to Be a Girly Girl in
Just Ten Days

Ice Dreams

Juicy Gossip

Making Waves

Miss Popularity

Miss Popularity
Goes Camping

Miss Popularity
and the Best Friend Disaster

Totally Crushed

Wish You Were Here,
Liza

See You Soon,
Samantha

Miss You, Mina

Winner Takes All

POISON APPLE BOOKS

The Dead End

This Totally Bites!

Miss Fortune

Now You See Me...

Midnight Howl

Her Evil Twin

Curiosity Killed the Cat

At First Bite

THRILLING.
BONE-CHILLING.
THESE BOOKS
HAVE BITE!

Danny Shine just wants to draw comics,
buy comics, and talk about comics. But
first, he has to get his name off of

THE LOSER LIST

About Jim Benton

Jim Benton is not a middle-school girl, but do not hold that against him. He has managed to make a living out of being funny, anyway.

He is the creator of many licensed properties, some for big kids, some for little kids, and some for grown-ups who, frankly, are probably behaving like little kids.

You may already know his properties: It's Happy Bunny™ or Just Jimmy™, and of course you already know about Dear Dumb Diary.

He's created a kids' TV series, designed clothing, and written books.

Jim Benton lives in Michigan with his spectacular wife and kids. They do not have a dog, and they especially do not have a vengeful beagle. This is his first series for Scholastic.

Jamie Kelly has no idea that Jim Benton, or you, or anybody is reading her diaries. So, please, please, please don't tell her.